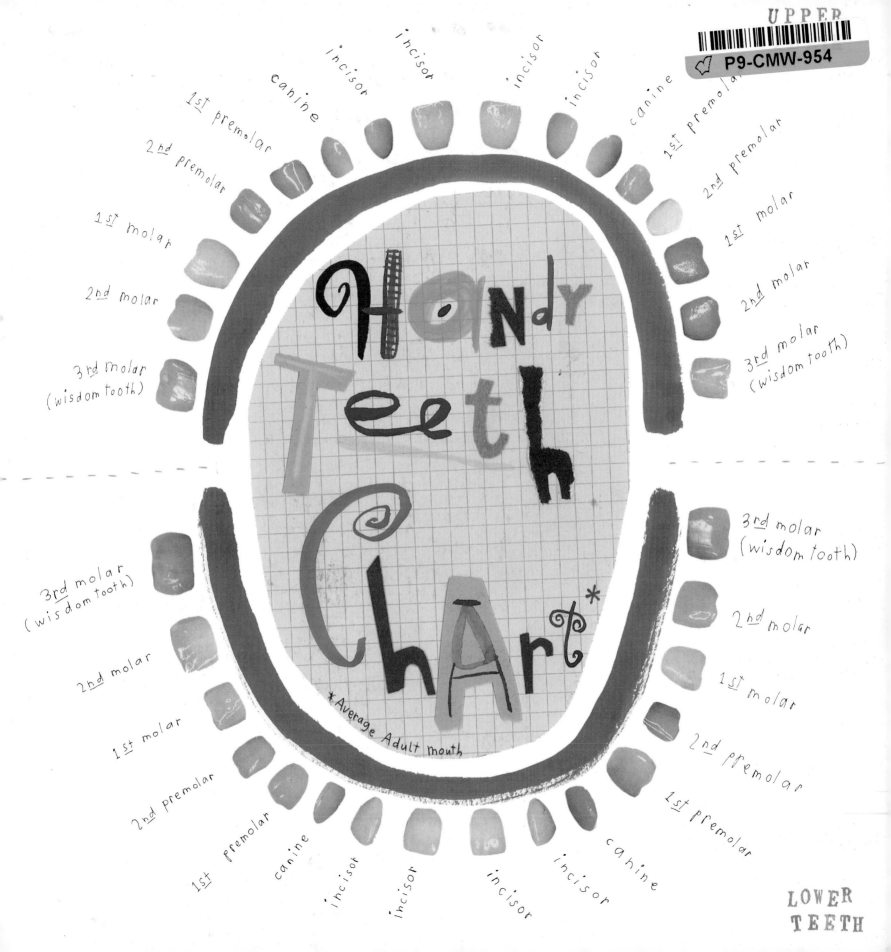

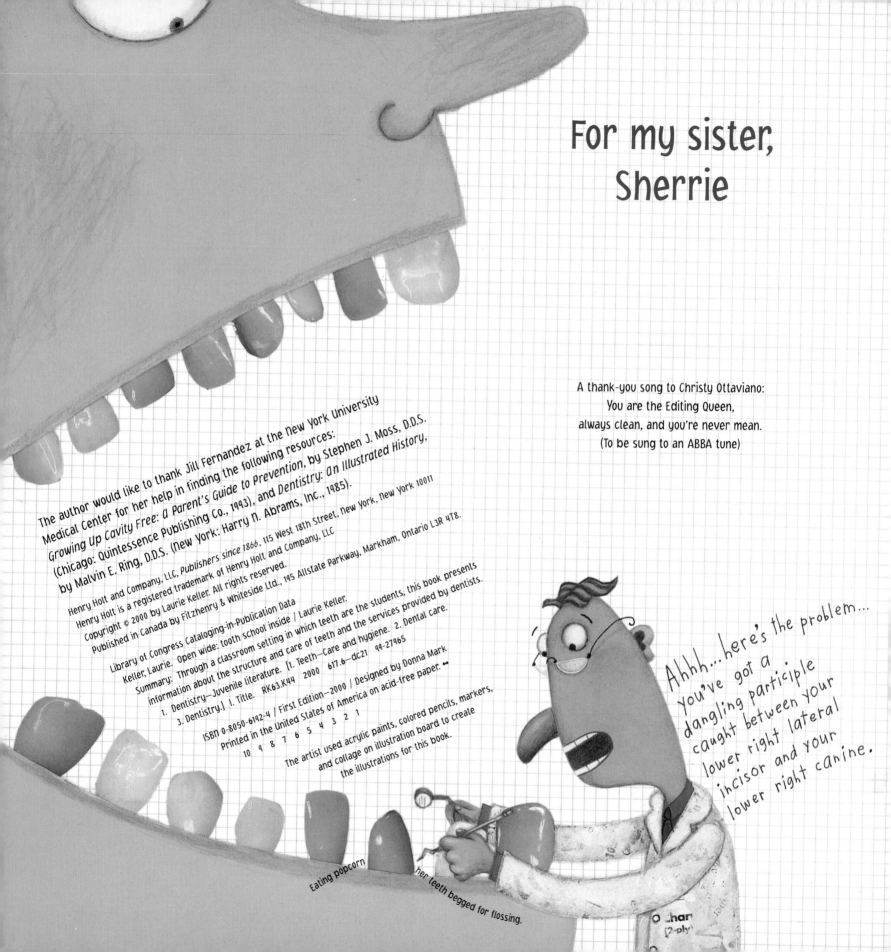

For my sister, Sherrie

A thank-you song to Christy Ottaviano:
You are the Editing Queen,
always clean, and you're never mean.
(To be sung to an ABBA tune)

The author would like to thank Jill Fernandez at the New York University Medical Center for her help in finding the following resources: *Growing Up Cavity Free: A Parent's Guide to Prevention*, by Stephen J. Moss, D.D.S. (Chicago: Quintessence Publishing Co., 1993), and *Dentistry: An Illustrated History*, by Malvin E. Ring, D.D.S. (New York: Harry N. Abrams, Inc., 1985).

Henry Holt and Company, LLC, *Publishers since 1866*, 115 West 18th Street, New York, New York 10011

Henry Holt is a registered trademark of Henry Holt and Company, LLC

Library of Congress Cataloging-in-Publication Data
Keller, Laurie. Open wide: tooth school inside / Laurie Keller.
Summary: Through a classroom setting in which teeth are the students, this book presents
information about the structure and care of teeth and the services provided by dentists.
1. Dentistry—Juvenile literature. [1. Teeth—Care and hygiene. 2. Dental care.
3. Dentistry.] I. Title. RK63.K44 2000 617.6—dc21 99-27965

ISBN 0-8050-6192-4 / First Edition—2000 / Designed by Donna Mark
Printed in the United States of America on acid-free paper. ∞
10 9 8 7 6 5 4 3 2 1

The artist used acrylic paints, colored pencils, markers,
and collage on illustration board to create
the illustrations for this book.

Ahhh...here's the problem... You've got a dangling participle caught between your lower right lateral incisor and your lower right canine.

Eating popcorn her teeth begged for flossing.

Good morning, class.

Good morning, Dr. Flossman!

upper teeth
lower teeth

You're all looking clean and bright today. Let's begin by taking attendance.

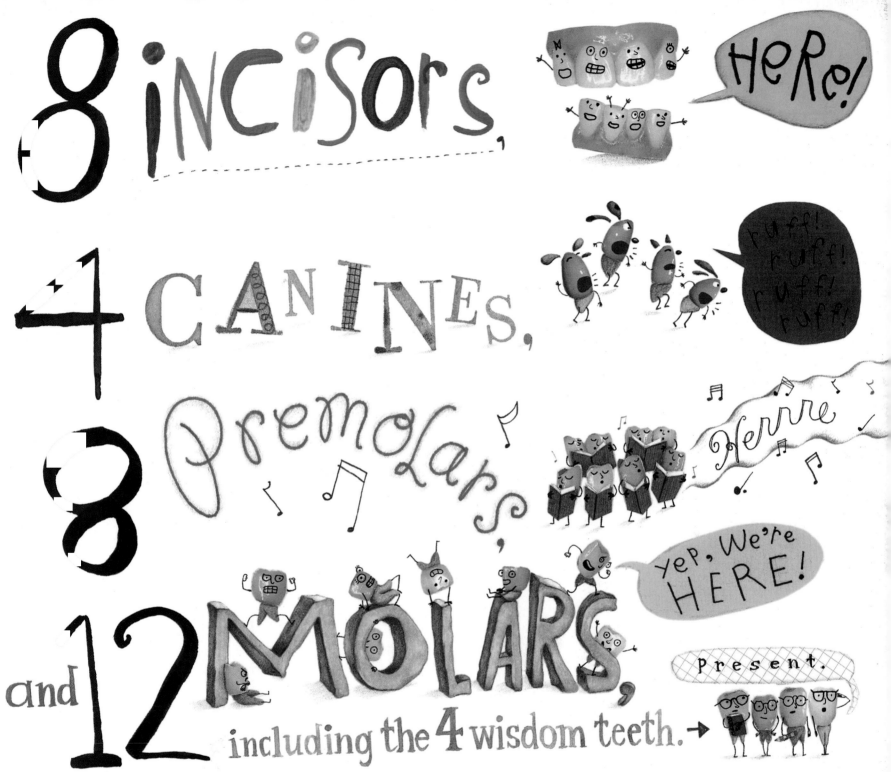

8 incisors,

4 canines,

premolars,

and 12 molars,

including the 4 wisdom teeth. →

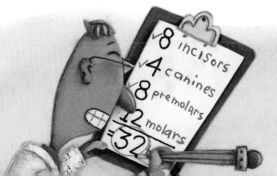

Oh goody gumdrops—
all **32** of you are here!

Before the principal's announcements, would you all please stand and recite our pledge:

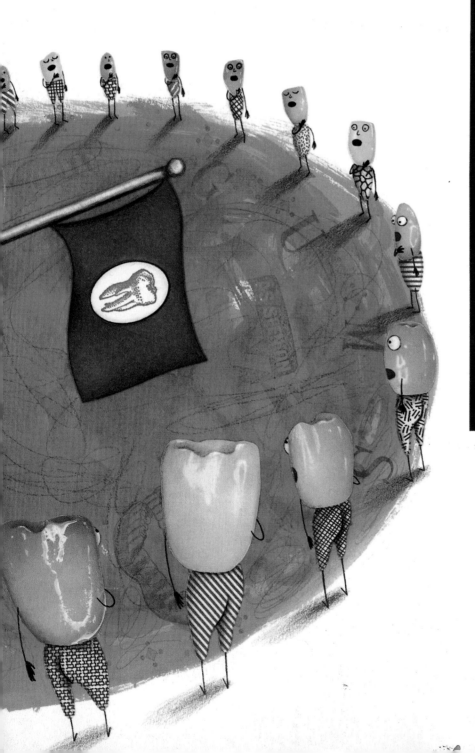

I pledge allegiance to this mouth and to the dentist who takes care of us. And to the gums on which we stand, strong and healthy, with toothbrushes and toothpaste for all.

I get choked up every time — give me just a minute...

Dentist's Manual

Take your seats, everyone. I'm handing back your quizzes from yesterday on what healthy teeth should look like. I must say, I'm a little disappointed—the only teeth who passed are the wisdom teeth. We better go over this again:

Shiny, clean teeth— GOOD.

Holey, green teeth— BAD.

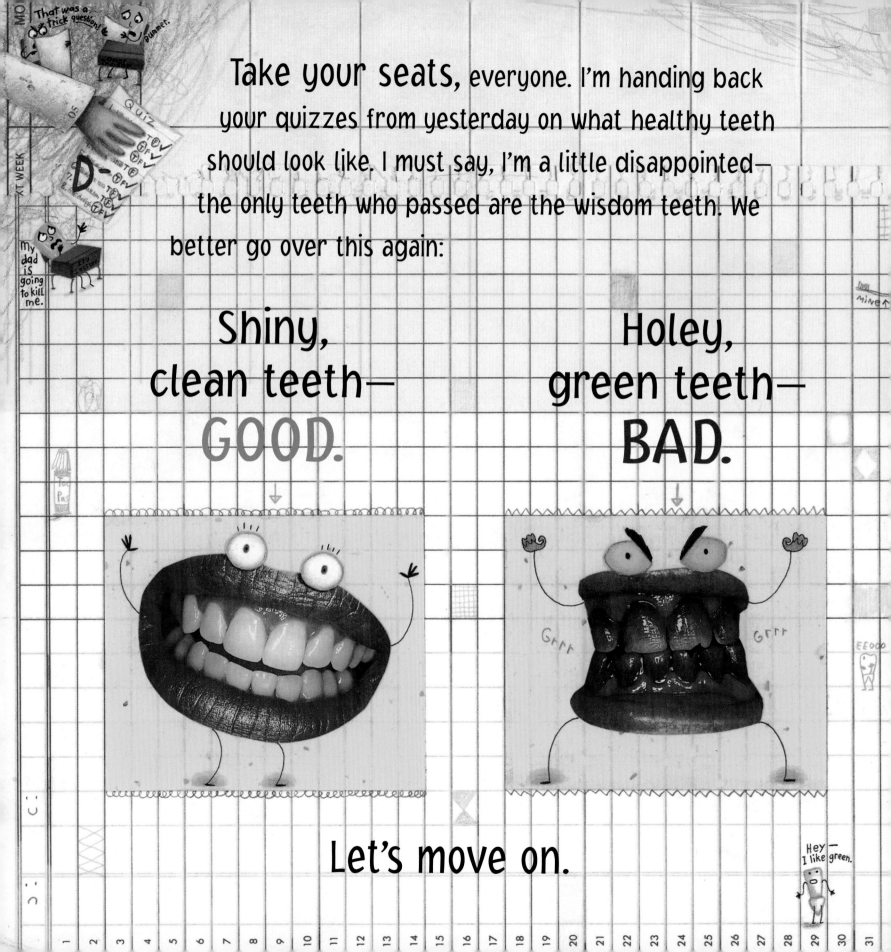

Let's move on.

Here's a look at what you teeth are made of:

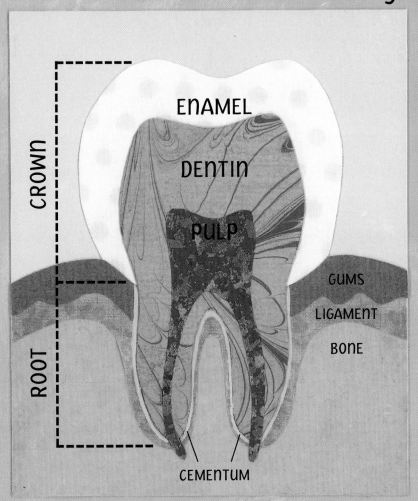

ENAMEL

DENTIN

PULP

CROWN

ROOT

GUMS

LIGAMENT

BONE

CEMENTUM

1. When you're in the gums, the part of you that shows is the CROWN.

How fancy.

2. You're covered with a hard layer of ENAMEL to protect you from bacteria and germs.

Did someone say germs?

3. DENTIN makes up the biggest part of you. It's not as hard as enamel.

Ohmmm

Getting in touch with inner dentin

4. PULP is the softest part. It's what hurts when you get a toothache.

Ouch.

5. The ROOT is what holds you in place. It's protected by a thin layer of tissue called CEMENTUM.

Guess I'm not going out tonight.

Bb Cc Dd Ee Ff Gg Hh Ii Jj Kk Ll Mm Nn Oo Pp Qq Rr

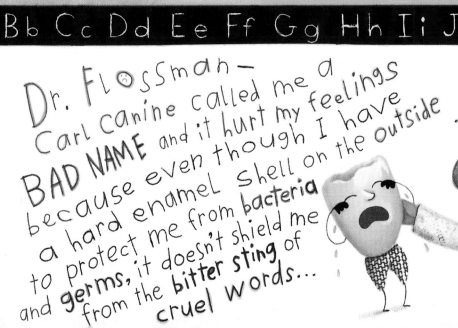

Dr. Flossman—
Carl Canine called me a BAD NAME and it hurt my feelings because even though I have a hard enamel shell on the outside to protect me from bacteria and germs, it doesn't shield me from the bitter sting of cruel words...

There, there, little molar.

Will we be tested on that stuff up there?

A Clean Tooth Is a Happy Toot

Okay, class. Now we're in for a REAL TREAT.

Sally Incisor is going to read her report on primary teeth.

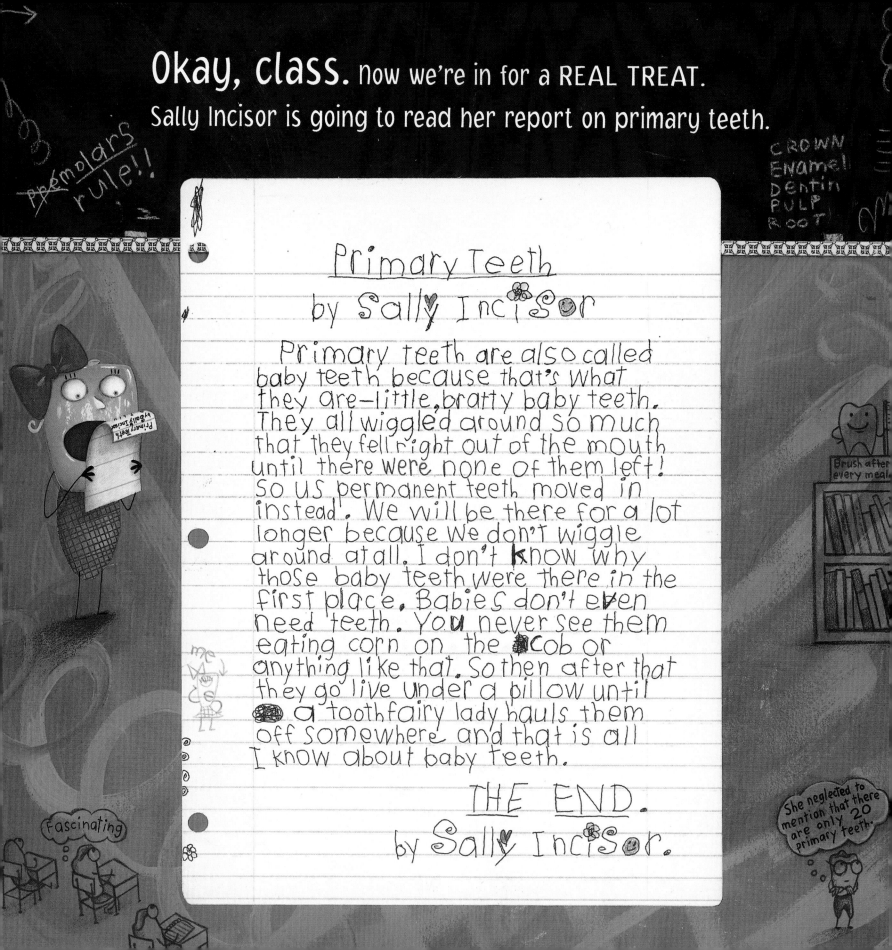

Primary Teeth
by Sally Incisor

Primary teeth are also called baby teeth because that's what they are—little, bratty baby teeth. They all wiggled around so much that they fell right out of the mouth until there were none of them left! So us permanent teeth moved in instead. We will be there for a lot longer because we don't wiggle around at all. I don't know why those baby teeth were there in the first place. Babies don't even need teeth. You never see them eating corn on the cob or anything like that. So then after that they go live under a pillow until a toothfairy lady hauls them off somewhere and that is all I know about baby teeth.

THE END.
by Sally Incisor.

premolars rule!!

CROWN
ENAMEL
DENTIN
PULP
ROOT

Brush after every meal

Fascinating

She neglected to mention that there are only 20 primary teeth.

me

Primary Teeth by Sally Incisor

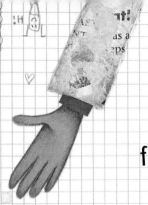

Thank you, Sally. Nice job! But actually, babies **DO** need teeth. Baby teeth are **VERY** important for several reasons.

1. They help develop the face and jaw.

2. They help babies chew when they start to eat more solid food.

3. And baby teeth guided you permanent teeth into proper position, and kept the mouth healthy and clean.

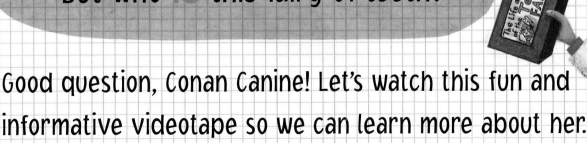

That's real swell, Doc. But who **is** this fairy of teeth?

Good question, Conan Canine! Let's watch this fun and informative videotape so we can learn more about her.

Hello there,
you cute little permanent teeth!

This is the Tooth Fairy coming to you all the way from Tooth Land. It's my job to bring all the baby teeth here. When a baby tooth falls out, it gets placed under a pillow (which I've never understood—I practically suffocate sometimes trying to get it). After I take the tooth, I replace it with a little surprise—usually money. Then I tuck the tooth under my wing and we're off to Tooth Land!

Well, that's about it for me. Oh—I almost forgot. There's free molar-coaster rides on Tuesday nights, so stop by!

Toodle-do, toothies!

FOOD CUTTERS

INCISORS

FOOD TEARERS

CANINES

FOOD CRUSHERS

PREMOLARS

FOOD GRINDERS

MOLARS

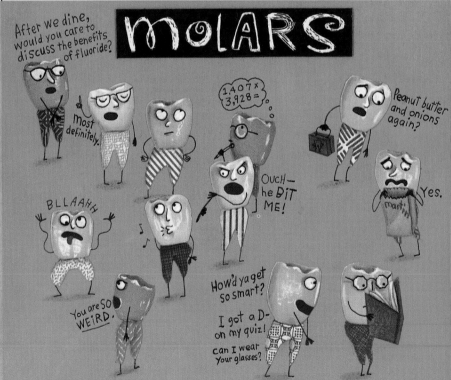

Way to go, class—get in there and **EAT!**

Well, well, well! It looks like you all had a good lunch. But to stay strong and healthy, it's important to brush after meals. So what do you say we take out our toothbrushes and floss, and clean ourselves up?

All right then, class. Since you don't want to brush, why don't we open our books to the chapter on TOOTH DECAY.

Tooth decay is caused by bacteria.
Bacteria like to eat sugar.
Candy and cookies have one
kind of sugar, and foods like
fruit, bread, pasta, and milk have other
kinds of sugar. Bacteria eat all kinds—
especially those that stick to teeth.

(Notice how some foods are not as sticky as they would seem to be.)

NOT VERY STICKY
apples
bananas
hot fudge sundaes

SORT OF STICKY
white bread
caramels
cream-filled sponge cake

PRETTY STICKY
jelly beans
plain doughnuts
raisins

SUPER STICKY
granola bars
oatmeal cookies
potato chips

When lots of bacteria build up on
teeth, that's known as PLAQUE.
Plaque eats right through enamel.
And if plaque keeps eating, it
means only one thing—

A CAVITY!

Oh, the HORROR of it all!

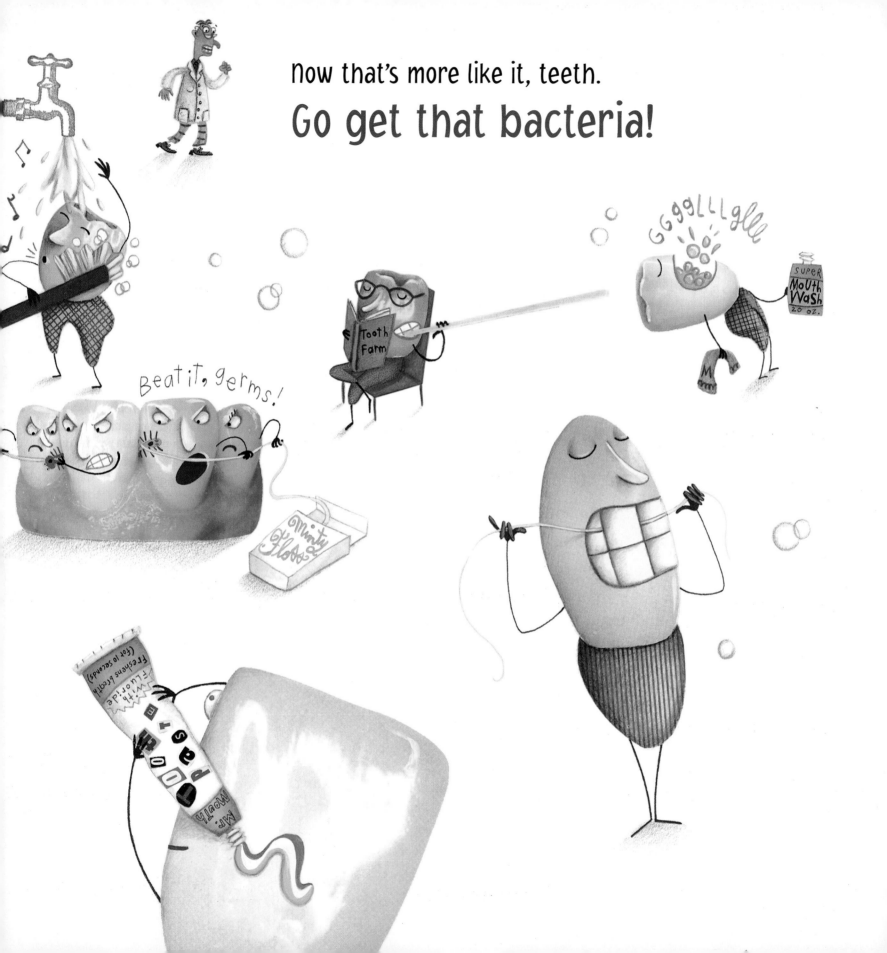

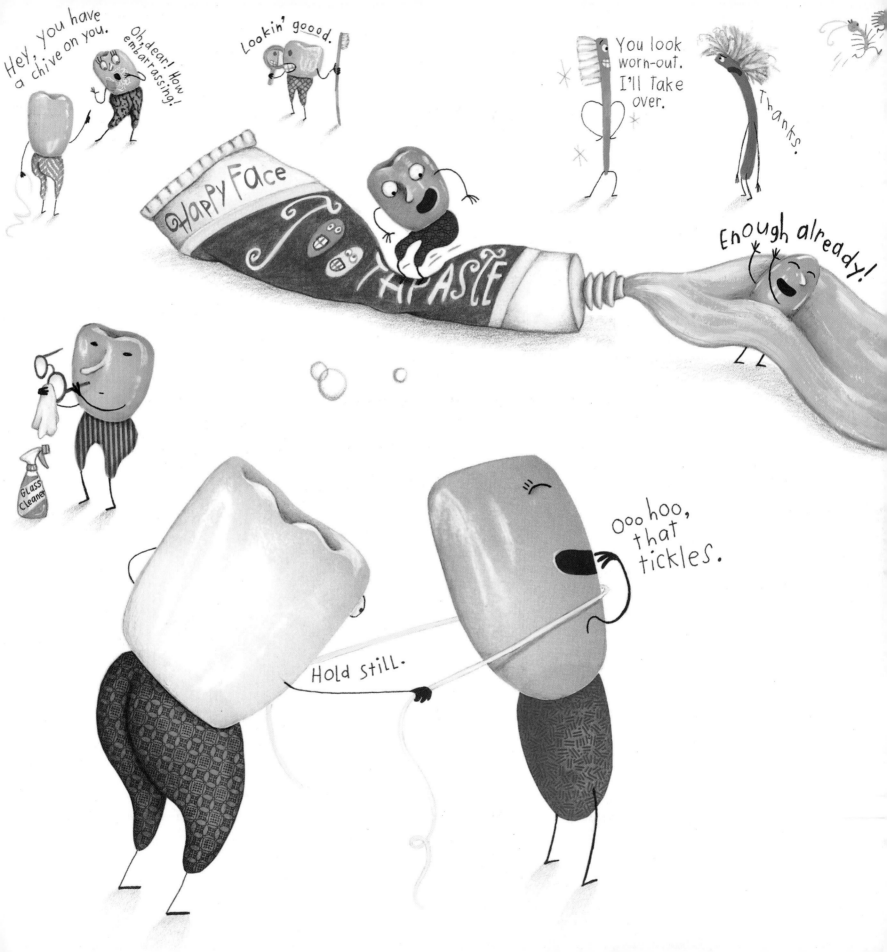

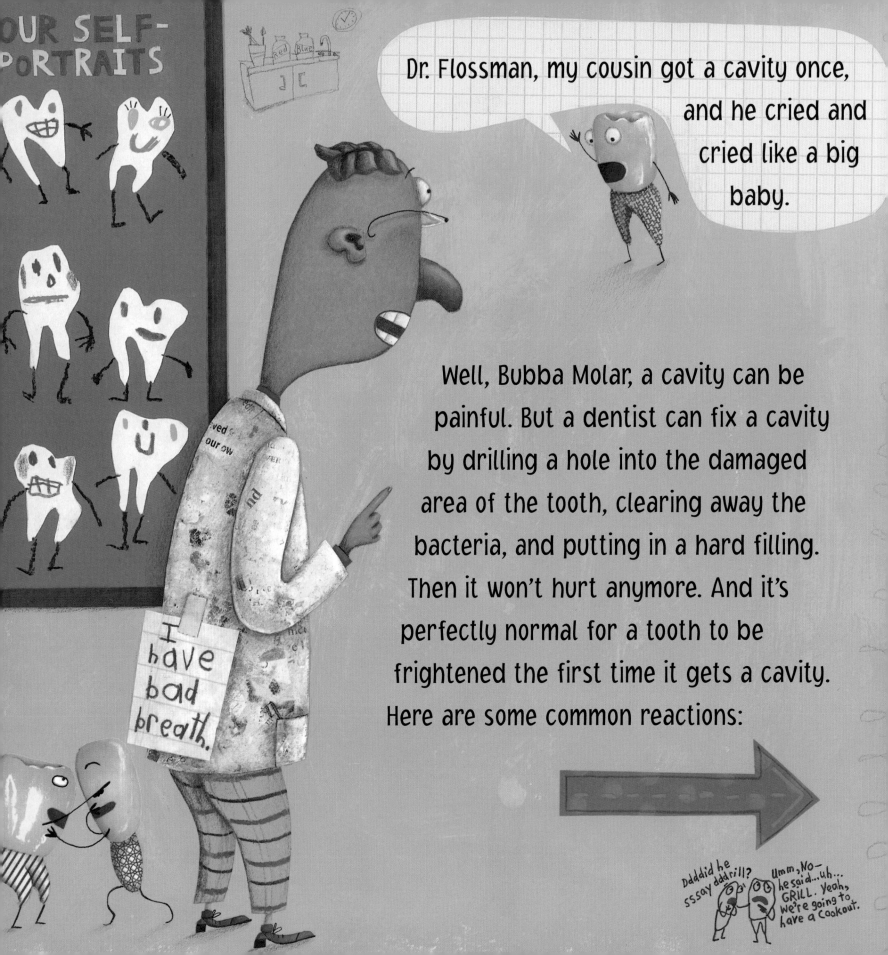

9 Common Reactions to Cavities*

SHOCK

PANIC

DEPRESSION

SELF-PITY
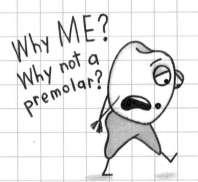

FEAR

ANGER

BLAME

DENIAL

ACCEPTANCE

*From the best-selling book *So You've Got Yourself a Cavity*, by Dr. Lou Stooth.

When a cavity is too small to see, a dentist will take an X RAY. An X ray can show the inside of a tooth. It makes cavities easy to see.

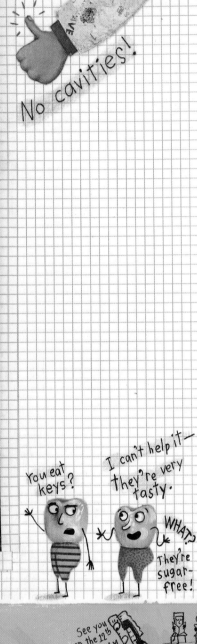

No cavities!

You eat keys?

I can't help it—they're very tasty.

WHAT? They're sugar-free!

See you on the 22ᵗʰ at 9:00 A.M., Mr. Tootharino.

Check the back.

Looks good.

Don't you worry, teeth—brushing with fluoride toothpaste and flossing keeps away most plaque. But you should visit the dentist once or twice a year for a checkup to make sure you're healthy and clean.

An important reminder about dentists:

A **GOOD** dentist cleans and polishes teeth, and gives them a new toothbrush.

A **BAD** dentist skips work to play golf and sends his brother, the construction worker, to take his place.

Sometimes, if teeth are CROOKED, a dentist will put braces on them to make them straight.

BEFORE

AFTER

Now I can suck your blood!

If a tooth gets BROKEN, a dentist can repair it with a tooth-colored plastic to make it look like new.

BEFORE

AFTER

Got any wood?

Toothpaste and paste are not the same!

T + ooth = Tooth →

Class, I need to speak to the wisdom teeth for a minute in the hallway, but when I get back be ready to give your reports on teeth throughout history.

Yes, Dr. Flossman

I'm back, class. So let's hear those reports.

Ancient Egyptians believed that a mixture of onion, spices, and incense would cure a toothache.

In the ninth century, Mayans filed their teeth into different shapes and decorated them with jewels.

In 1570, Queen Elizabeth received a gift of six gold toothpicks to clean her teeth.

In the early 1600s, Japanese women blackened their teeth to show loyalty to their husbands.

In the Middle Ages, Apollonia became the patron saint of dentistry. She said if someone with a toothache mentioned her name, the pain would go away.

In the 1500s, people could get their hair cut, wounds treated, and teeth pulled by their barber.

George Washington, the first president of the United States, had lots of dental problems. By 1796 he had lost all but one of his teeth. He had dentures made of elephant ivory, hippopotamus tusks, and cow teeth (not wood, as you may have heard). The dentures had sharp hooks, screws, and springs that made it hard for him to smile.

Excellent job, teeth! I'm so proud of you.

CLAP CLAP

For tomorrow:
Answer questions
in the back of
the book.

OFFICIAL DENTIST
DR. Flossman

RiiNN

Well, rinse, gargle, and spit in a cup!
We're done for the day, teeth, so
I'll see you back here tomorrow.
Now don't forget your homework.

And don't forget to brush!

True or False

1. Army soldiers protect teeth from bacteria and germs.   T or F

2. Healthy teeth should be holey and green.   T or F

3. Baby teeth guide permanent teeth into position.   T or F

4. Fruit, bread, pasta, and milk have sugar in them.   T or F

5. Bacteria like to eat sugar.   T or F

6. A dentist can fix a cavity by putting a bandage on it and giving it a kiss.   T or F

7. Teeth should have a checkup once or twice a year by a mechanic.   T or F

8. An X ray can show the inside of a tooth.   T or F

9. George Washington had teeth made out of rocks and twigs.   T or F

10. Marshmallow is the softest part of the tooth.   T or F

What did you get for number two?

True or False Answers:

1. F; 2. F; 3. T; 4. T; 5. T; 6. F; 7. F; 8. T; 9. F; 10. F

Multiple Choice

1. How many permanent teeth are in the mouth?

   a. 4   b. 32   c. 97

2. What holds teeth in place?

   a. a root   b. a boot   c. a parachute

3. Primary teeth are also known as

   a. grumpy teeth   b. baby teeth   c. smelly teeth

4. The incisors are

   a. food throwers   b. food wasters   c. food cutters

5. After meals teeth should be

   a. painted purple   b. brushed and   c. pulled out and
                              flossed   put back in

6. Tooth decay is caused by

   a. bacteria and   b. slugs and   c. bad perms
      germs   worms

7. If plaque builds up on teeth it can cause

   a. a thunderstorm   b. a fight   c. a cavity

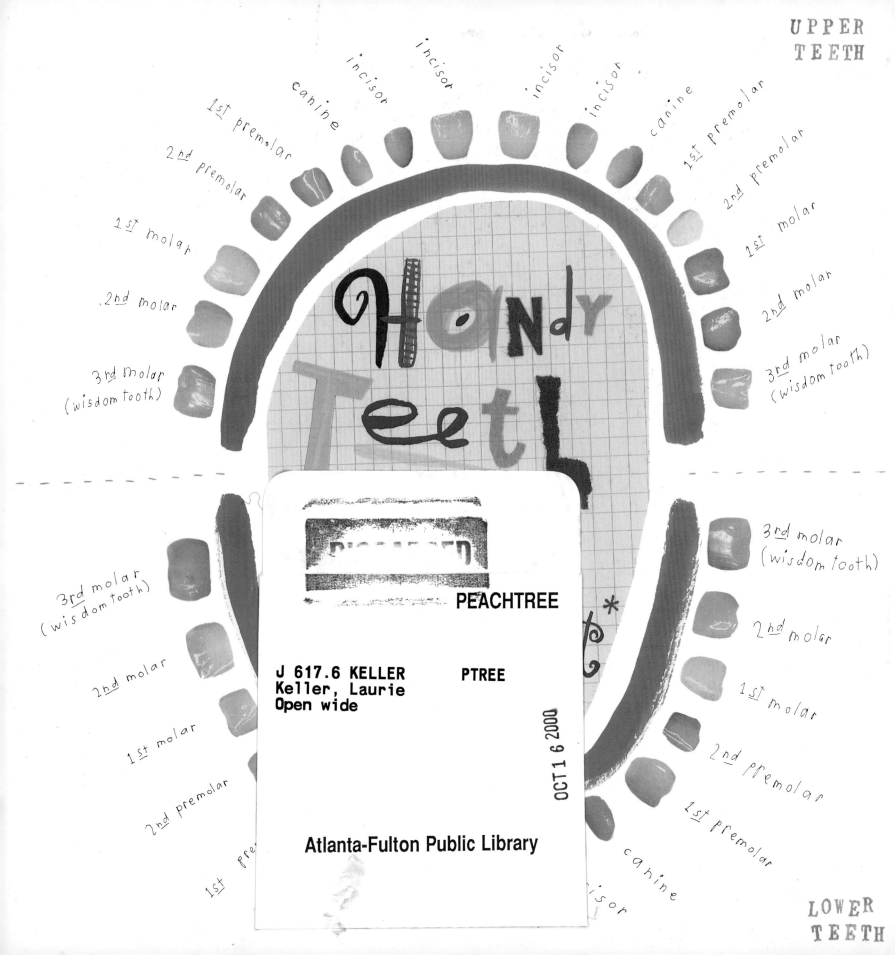

incisor

incisor

incisor

incisor

canine

canine

1st premolar

1st premolar

2nd premolar

2nd premolar

1st molar

1st molar

2nd molar

2nd molar

3rd molar
(wisdom tooth)

3rd molar
(wisdom tooth)

Handy Teeth

3rd molar
(wisdom tooth)

3rd molar
(wisdom tooth)

2nd molar

2nd molar

1st molar

1st molar

2nd premolar

2nd premolar

1st premolar

1st premolar

canine

incisor